Easter B
Amazing Egg Machine

MW01062545

For David J. Lewison, an egg-ceptional machine designer and son.—W.C.L.

For my children and yours, with a renewed value of life.—N.C., October 2001

By Wendy Cheyette Lewison • Illustrated by Normand Chartier

A Random House PICTUREBACK® Book

Random House New York

Text copyright © 2002 by Wendy Cheyette Lewison. Illustrations copyright © 2002 by Normand Chartier. All rights reserved under International and Pan-American Copyright Conventions. Published in the United States by Random House, Inc., New York, and simultaneously in Canada by Random House of Canada Limited, Toronto. www.randomhouse.com/kids

Library of Congress Cataloging-in-Publication Data: Lewison, Wendy Cheyette. Easter Bunny's amazing egg machine / by Wendy Cheyette Lewison ; illustrated by Normand Chartier. p. cm. — (A Random House pictureback) Summary: Easter Bunny is too sick to dye all the Easter eggs in time, so he creates a machine to help. ISBN 0-375-81263-6 [1. Easter—Fiction. 2. Rabbits—Fiction. 3. Easter eggs—Fiction. 4. Sick—Fiction. 5. Inventions—Fiction. 6. Friendship—Fiction.] I. Chartier, Normand, 1945– ill. II. Title. III. Series.
PZ7.L5884 Eas 2002 [E]—dc21 2001019925

Printed in the United States of America First Edition January 2002 10 9 8 7 6 5 4 3 2 1

PICTUREBACK, RANDOM HOUSE, PLEASE READ TO ME, and colophons are registered trademarks of Random House, Inc.

Easter Bunny was in bed with a bad case of the flu. In his workshop, eggs were waiting to be colored—but all Easter Bunny could do was sniffle and sneeze and say, "Oh, my head! Ooh, my stomach!"

APRIL

To cheer him up, his friends brought him carrot soup.

They made him
"Get well soon, Easter Bunny" cards.

After a while, Easter Bunny began to feel a little bit better. "I must get to work!" he exclaimed, and started coloring eggs as fast as he could.

"Let us help," suggested the mole twins.

"Thank you," said Easter Bunny. "But I can do it—*achoo!*—myself."

For days and days, Easter Bunny colored eggs.

At last, it was just one day before Easter.

"Oh, dear," said Easter Bunny. "These eggs will never be ready in time!"

He had to speed things up. But how?

Suddenly an amazing idea popped into Easter Bunny's head, an idea full of thing-a-ma-jigs and what-cha-ma-call-its.

He drew a picture of it, then hopped around the house, gathering together building materials.

And after a lot of clinking and clanging and rattling and banging—there it was . . .

. . . an Easter egg machine!

"This machine will make Easter eggs faster than the Easter Bunny himself," chuckled Easter Bunny.

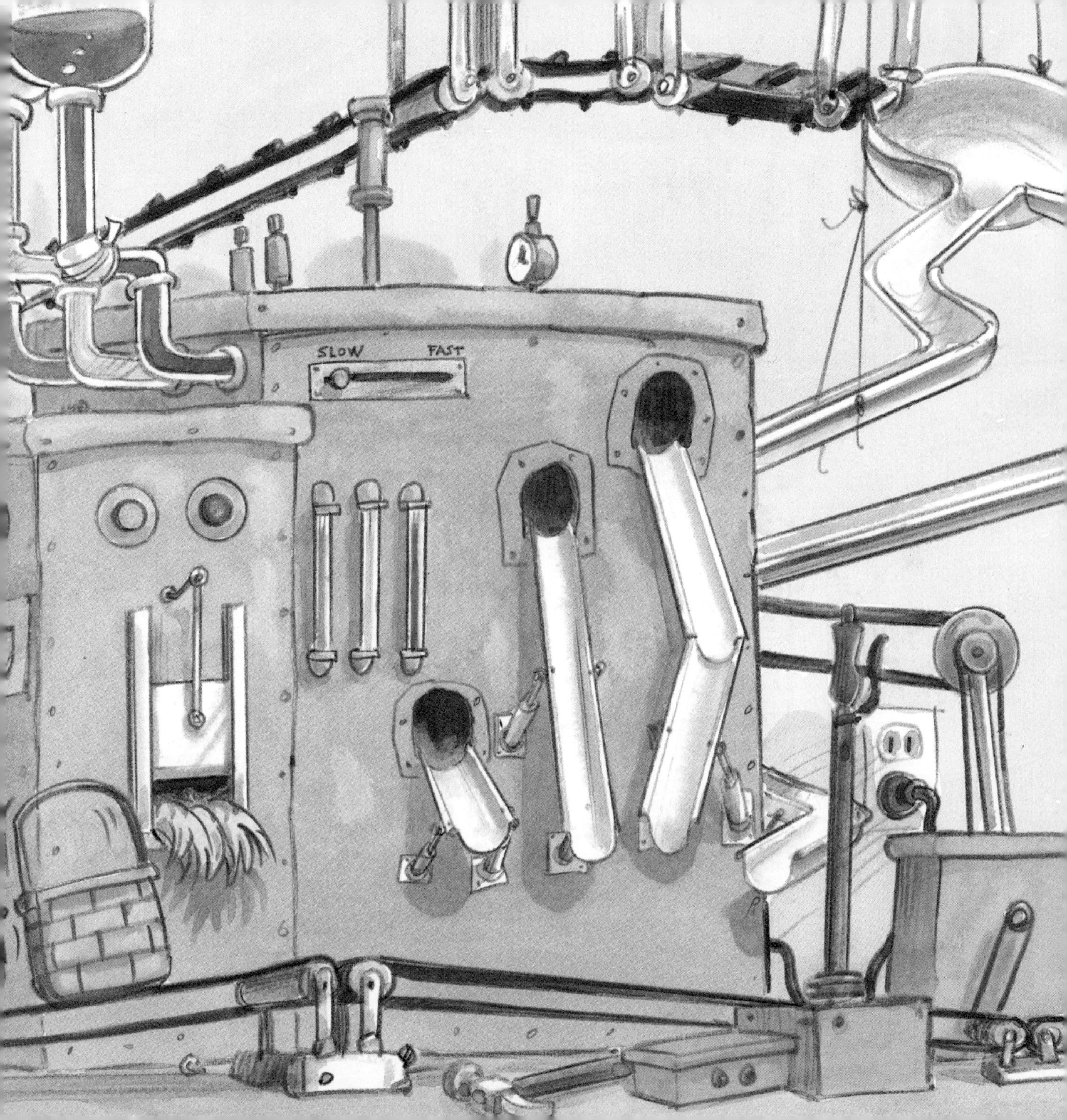
SLOW
FAST

Easter Bunny wanted to try it out right away. So he took a plain white egg and placed it on the belt. Then he pushed the green button.

The machine began to whirr and buzz. Then the egg disappeared inside the machine.

Easter Bunny raced around to the other side. *Pop!* The plain white egg had become bright orange—a perfect Easter egg!

"I'll be done with my eggs in no time at all!" said Easter Bunny.

He began feeding the eggs into the machine. *Zip!* As soon as he put them in, out they came at the other end. *Pop!*

Blue eggs and pink eggs. Yellow eggs and purple eggs. Striped eggs and dotted eggs. Eggs with zigzag designs and eggs with flowers all around. There were even eggs with cute little bunnies on them.

Easter Bunny hopped back and forth, filling up baskets with pretty Easter eggs. The egg machine worked beautifully—even better than he had imagined.

So Easter Bunny began to put the eggs in faster—*zip, zip, zip.* Out they came, just as fast—*pop, pop, pop.*

Until . . .

SLOW
FAST
POP
POP
Pop
POP
ZiP
Zip
Zip

. . . *Clunk!*

"What was that?" said Easter Bunny. He stopped in his tracks to listen. . . .

Clunk, clunk. Clunk, CLUNK!

All of a sudden, the machine speeded up. Strange-looking eggs started popping out. Eggs with whiskers. Eggs with tails. Eggs that looked like baseballs and soccer balls. Square eggs. Eggs with wings. Even scrambled eggs!

Before Easter Bunny could pull the plug, eggs were flying everywhere. They hit the ceiling, the walls, the floor. They hit the windows, the doors, the furniture. One uncooked egg landed right on Easter Bunny's head. *Splat!*

Several eggs even flew into the fireplace, up the chimney, and out into the moonlit garden. Outside, Easter Bunny's animal friends watched in amazement. What could be going on in Easter Bunny's workshop?

They opened the door. There was Easter Bunny, wiping his face.

"This is terrible!" cried Easter Bunny. "Easter will be here in just a few hours, and I don't have nearly enough Easter eggs to hide for the children."

"Then what are we waiting for?" said the mole twins.

The chipmunks and moles cleaned up the mess. The hens laid eggs. The birds colored and decorated them.

Just before the sun rose on Easter morning, Easter Bunny hid the Easter eggs one by one. Under the rosebush, by the garden gate, behind some rocks—until there were only a few eggs left in his basket. Easter Bunny knew just what he was going to do with those extra eggs. . . .

"I'll take these home," he said, "for my extra-special friends!"